Ladybird books are widely available, but in case of
difficulty may be ordered by post or telephone from:

Ladybird Books – Cash Sales Department
Littlegate Road Paignton Devon TQ3 3BE
Telephone 0803 554761

A catalogue record for this book is available
from the British Library

Published by Ladybird Books Ltd Loughborough Leicestershire UK
Ladybird Books Inc Auburn Maine 04210 USA

Printed in EC

DESPERATE DAN

AND THE CACTUSMAN

Ladybird

Desperate Dan needed a break. He was used to breaking things, but having a break himself – now that was a different matter! Dan sure loved the outdoors, so he'd decided to get away from it all in the desert.

"This is the life," sighed Dan as he climbed into his extra-large sleeping bag. "Twinklin' stars above, an' nothin' but peace an' quiet. This is gonna make me feel HEAPS better!"

Dan was mighty tired.

"Ah could sleep for days!" he yawned. And he started right away, surrounded in the silent desert by all the beautiful cactuses.

But wait! One of the cactuses – did it move?

Yes, it did! That's because it wasn't a cactus at all. It was one of Dan's dreaded, evil enemies – the Abominable Cactusman! So much for peace and quiet...

ZZZ!

Now, Dan was heavy. He was also a heavy sleeper, and he didn't stir in the slightest when the Cactusman stretched his arms towards Dan so that his spikes shot out like a porcupine's.

"Gosh, darn it, Aunt Aggie! Ah want bigger cow-pies than that!" shouted Dan in his sleep. He didn't notice that his sleeping bag had been pinned to the ground!

Quick as a flash, the Abominable Cactusman jumped onto Dan's famous road roller bike and sped off in the direction of Cactusville. Oh dear! There was trouble ahead...

Dan's dream made him hungry – he just had to have a midnight feast! But when he woke up he found that he'd been pinned to the spot.

"What in the name of tarnation?" grumbled Dan. "Ah came here for forty winks, not forty spikes! I reckon that creepy Cactusman's been makin' a nuisance of himself."

Dan took in a big gulp of air, swelled his chest, and then... POP! POP! POP! The spikes shot out like a flurry of arrows, leaving Dan with the world's first air-conditioned sleeping bag!

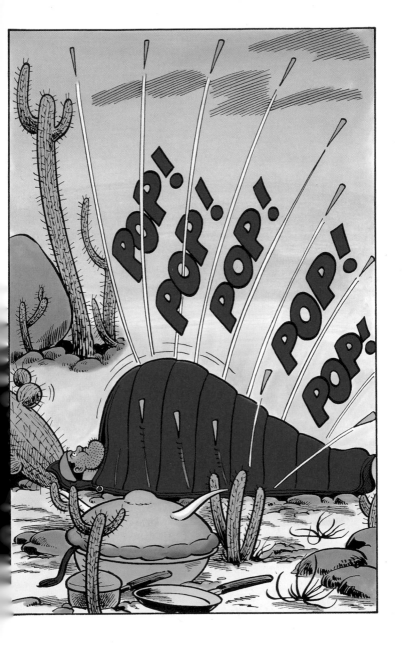

When Desperate Dan looked round, he saw the Abominable Cactusman pedalling away in the distance.

"That varmint! Ah knew it was him!" Dan growled. "He's gonna pay for ruining my beauty sleep!"

Just then, a farmer in his horse-drawn cart passed by. He happened to be heading for Cactusville, so, much to the horse's horror, Dan hitched a lift.

"Gasp!" wheezed the horse.

Oh dear! Dan was much too heavy to be pulled. But then he came up with the perfect solution.

"Don't you worry, poor horsey!" Dan smiled, as he unfastened the horse and set him down on the passenger seat. "You just stay there –'cause DAN'S gonna pull the wagon!"

The farmer was just as pleased as the horse – with Dan up front he'd get to Cactusville that much quicker!

Over in Cactusville, the Abominable Cactusman was already up to his prickly pranks. He'd jabbed the newspaper boy, scattering his papers everywhere.

"Spread the news, boy!" he cackled.

The painful pest had spiked the postman as well, sending his letters flying – even the ones that weren't marked 'AIR MAIL'!

When Dan got to town, he saw that the Abominable Cactusman had got straight to work. There was paper flying everywhere.

"That pesky critter – he's spreading litter!" fumed Dan. He wanted to get that green-skinned terror and teach him a lesson.

The trouble was, in a town full of cactuses it was extremely hard to find the Cactusman!

Just at that moment, Dan's Aunt Aggie walked by. She was carrying a snack-sized, fresh cow-pie.

"Another person to menace," thought the Cactusman, and he jabbed her like the others. A big mistake! Aunt Aggie dropped the cow-pie, ruining it completely. And if there's anything Desperate Dan can't stand, it's wasted cow-pie.

"Grrrr!" growled Dan, as he watched steam pouring from the broken pie.

"That no good, mischief-making, lame-brained excuse for a cactus!" boomed Dan, breathing in enough air to blow up a hot-air balloon, and whooshing the Cactusman clean off his feet.

"Urgh! Oof!" gasped the Cactusman.

Bull's-eye! Dan had pinned him onto the livery stable door.

The Abominable Cactusman was stuck to the wood by his own spikes and he couldn't break free. It isn't good to be stuck somewhere when Dan's really angry.

Desperate Dan, still steaming with rage, didn't say a word.

"Mercy!" pleaded the Cactusman. "I'll do anything you want! I'll even make up for all the bad that I've done! Just don't hurt me, okay?"

"So you want to make up for everythin', eh?" said Dan. "I'm gonna take you up on that!" And, tearing him from the stable door, he set the Cactusman rolling down the street.

Dan's Cactusville friends cheered as the pesky troublemaker's spikes picked up all the litter.

"I ought to take you for a spin more often!" laughed Dan.

But the Cactusman certainly wasn't smiling. He felt so ill from the spinning that if he wasn't that colour already, his skin would have gone as green as a desert cactus!